Dear Parent:

Psst . . . you're looking at the Super Secret Weapon of Reading. It's called comics.

STEP INTO READING® COMIC READERS are a perfect step in learning to read. They provide visual cues to the meaning of words and helpfully break out short pieces of dialogue into speech balloons.

Here are some terms commonly associated with comics:
  PANEL: A section of a comic with a box drawn around it.
  CAPTION: Narration that helps set the scene.
  SPEECH BALLOON: A bubble containing dialogue.
  GUTTER: The space between panels.

Tips for reading comics with your child:

• Have your child read the speech balloons while you read the captions.
• Ask your child: What is a character feeling? How can you tell?
• Have your child draw a comic showing what happens after the book is finished.

STEP INTO READING® COMIC READERS are designed to engage and to provide an empowering reading experience. They are also fun. The best-kept secret of comics is that they create lifelong readers. And that will make you the real hero of the story!

Jenni — M.Holm

Jennifer L. Holm and Matthew Holm
Co-creators of the Babymouse and Squish series

For Mima, Papa, Grandma, and Grandpa —J.F.

Copyright © 2017 by Jonathan Fenske

All rights reserved. Published in the United States by Random House Children's Books, a division of Penguin Random House LLC, New York. Originally published in hardcover in the United States by Penguin Young Readers, an imprint of Penguin Random House LLC, New York, in 2017.

Step into Reading, Random House, and the Random House colophon are registered trademarks of Penguin Random House LLC.

Visit us on the Web!
StepIntoReading.com
rhcbooks.com

Educators and librarians, for a variety of teaching tools, visit us at
RHTeachersLibrarians.com

Library of Congress Cataloging-in-Publication Data is available upon request.
ISBN 978-0-593-43262-4 (trade) — ISBN 978-0-593-43263-1 (lib. bdg.)

Printed in the United States of America
10 9 8 7 6 5 4 3 2 1

This book has been officially leveled by using the F&P Text Level Gradient™ Leveling System.

A PIG, A FOX, AND STINKY SOCKS

by Jonathan Fenske

Random House 🏠 New York

PART ONE

5

And hide inside this handy pail.

To watch Pig find his stinky mail.

13

PART TWO

16

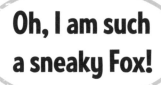

18

Another pair of socks that stink.
Another funny trick I think.

19

21

Here comes Pig! I must be quick!

This empty can should do the trick.

24

27

PART THREE

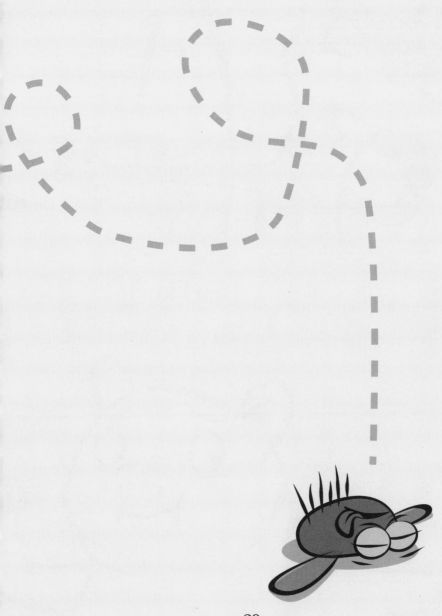